Galileo's Treasure Box

♦ CATHERINE BRIGHTON ♦

Introduction by Dava Sobel

Walker & Company
NEW YORK

This book is dedicated to the
memory of Virginia Galilei, 1600–1634

The author would like to thank
Dr. Willem D. Hackmann, Assistant Curator,
Museum of the History of Science,
University of Oxford, for his help and advice.

◆ ◆ ◆

Originally published as *Five Secrets in a Box* in Great Britain in 1987 by Methuen
Children's Books Ltd; first published in the United States of America by E.P. Dutton.
This edition published in 2001 by Walker Publishing Company.

The right of Catherine Brighton to be identified as the Author of this Work
has been asserted in accordance with the Copyright Designs and Patents Act 1988.

Published simultaneously in Canada by Fitzhenry and
Whiteside, Markham, Ontario L3R 4T8

Library of Congress Cataloging-in-Publication Data

Brighton, Catherine.
    [Five secrets in a box]
    Galileo's treasure box/Catherine Brighton.
        p. cm.
    Summary: While Galileo sleeps, his young daughter Virginia, later known as Maria
Celeste, explores his study and discovers some of the tools he uses in his scientific experiments.
    ISBN 0-8027-8768-1 -- ISBN 0-8027-8770-3
    1. Galilei, Maria Celeste, 1600-1634--Juvenile fiction. [1. Galilei, Maria Celeste,
1600-1634--Fiction. 2. Galileo, 1564-1642--Fiction. 3. Fathers and daughters--Fiction.] I.
Title

    PZ7.B76524 Gal 2001
    [E]--dc21   2001022248

Book design by Rosanne Kakos-Main

Printed in Hong Kong

2 4 6 8 10 9 7 5 3 1

Introduction
Dava Sobel

Galileo's daughter came to Catherine Brighton in a waking dream. The child's curiosity, her intelligence, her sweetness, her respectful love for her father—all these qualities bring a relatively unknown historical figure to life for young readers.

Galileo's daughter Virginia, who became a cloistered nun, lovingly supported him from the peak of his scientific renown through his trial for heresy. But what was Virginia like as a girl? No records survive to tell how she spent her younger days—whether she went to school, or how often she stayed up late with her father looking through the telescope at the night sky.

Only nine years old when her father perfected his telescope, Virginia might well have touched and played with the simple treasures depicted in these richly detailed paintings—the curved polished lenses that Galileo set into lead tubes to view the planets and stars, the squat microscope he built to study insects, the measuring instruments he crafted out of brass or blown glass, the papers and journals he filled with his observations, the books he read and wrote. A single feather, dropped by the Grand Duke's falcon or some ordinary pigeon at the window, was enough to set him thinking productively about the forces that drive the universe.

As Virginia comes upon each of these objects, the most ordinary things begin to seem extraordinary. The magic of Catherine Brighton's book is the creation of a wonderful place where a child can play with the very tools an adult uses to understand the laws of nature.

My name is Virginia.
I am the daughter of Galileo.
My father studies the skies at night.
I sleep.

In the day he sleeps behind a fine curtain.
Our house is quiet.
My silent slippers creep.

My afternoon seems long.
I rustle to his study, up wide stone stairs.

His desk is covered with things.
I look, but I don't touch.
His papers. His instruments.

There is a box.
I lift the lid.
I peep inside.
There are five things in the box.

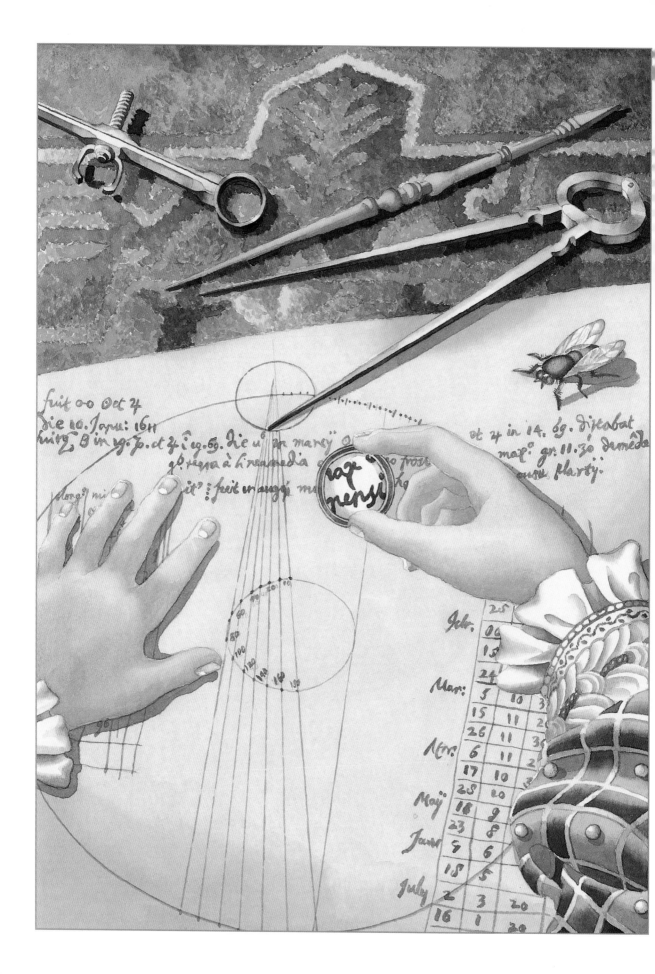

Two clear pieces of glass.
One round piece makes things bigger.
Look at his writing!

I hold the first piece next to the second.
The countryside comes toward me.
I see the children in the bell tower!
I see the golden oriole!

There are also pieces of colored glass in the box.
One is blue.
The world turns to night.

This red glass sets the world on fire.
The prince's falcon flies to the lure.

Last in the box is a feather.
Soft and white.
Why does my father keep a feather?

I go to him.
He is awake.
His book slips to the floor.
The feather floats after it.
He says the feather is important to his work.

I pick up the feather and he puts it in my hair.
I parade like a proud bird all day.
Galileo sleeps.

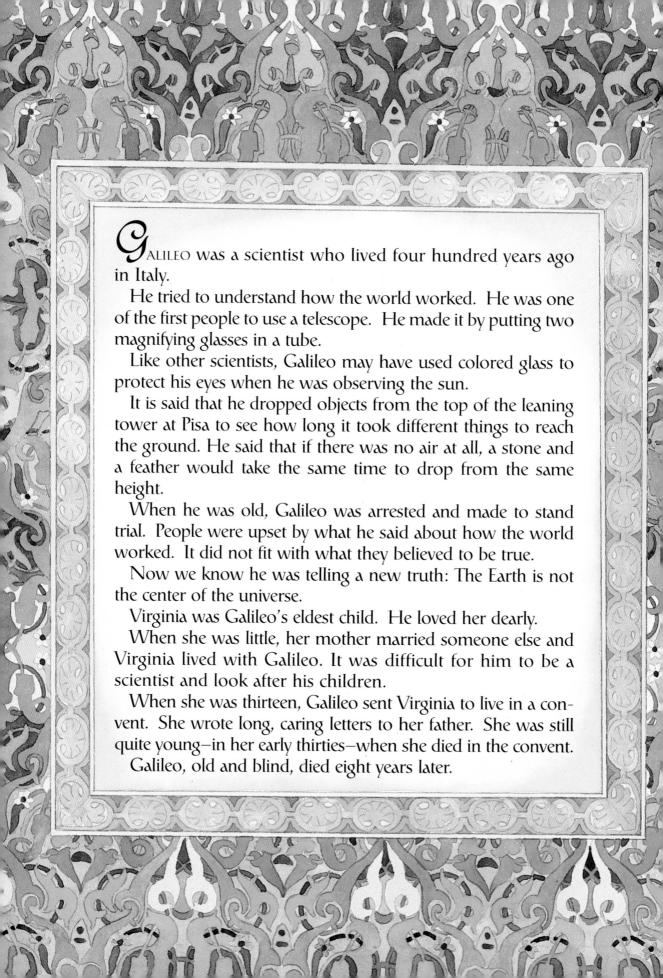

GALILEO was a scientist who lived four hundred years ago in Italy.

He tried to understand how the world worked. He was one of the first people to use a telescope. He made it by putting two magnifying glasses in a tube.

Like other scientists, Galileo may have used colored glass to protect his eyes when he was observing the sun.

It is said that he dropped objects from the top of the leaning tower at Pisa to see how long it took different things to reach the ground. He said that if there was no air at all, a stone and a feather would take the same time to drop from the same height.

When he was old, Galileo was arrested and made to stand trial. People were upset by what he said about how the world worked. It did not fit with what they believed to be true.

Now we know he was telling a new truth: The Earth is not the center of the universe.

Virginia was Galileo's eldest child. He loved her dearly.

When she was little, her mother married someone else and Virginia lived with Galileo. It was difficult for him to be a scientist and look after his children.

When she was thirteen, Galileo sent Virginia to live in a convent. She wrote long, caring letters to her father. She was still quite young–in her early thirties–when she died in the convent.

Galileo, old and blind, died eight years later.